UNCLE ALFREDO'S ZOO

by Judith Vigna

ALBERT WHITMAN & COMPANY • MORTON GROVE, ILLINOIS

THE JOURNEY FROM AMERICA TO ITALY had been long. A train, a plane, and then a train again.

It was January, the day before the Blessing of the Animals. And Anna and Nonna were in Cantalone at last.

"There," said Nonna, pointing to the hill above the station. "My uncle lived in that shepherd's hut, right outside the village. He and Mamma and Papa are dead now, but you will see Uncle Alfredo's zoo, just as I last saw it when I was a girl."

Anna could hardly wait.

Back in her grandmother's house in Connecticut, she had longingly touched the old gray photographs of stones. Now she would touch the stones themselves. Smooth snakestone, rough rhinostone, round owlstone, sleek tigerstone — stones carved by rain and wind into strange and wonderful creature-shapes. Uncle Alfredo had collected them to fill the nooks and crannies of his hut and sit on its garden walls.

A stone zoo, Nonna called it.

"Remember what I told you?" Nonna said now. "Almost all his life, as he watched his flock, my uncle hunted for stones. He hauled them from crags and peaks, some in his wooden litter, some on his back.

"And those too sunk in the ground, his sheepdog, Papite, dug, clawing them out with his big paws. Creature by creature the stone zoo grew, until it rivaled any real one. People came from everywhere to see it!"

It was so cold the taxi wouldn't start.

An old man said, "I'm going your way." His words were muffled by the thick cloak that hid his face, but Anna knew Italian and understood. His hands shook as he helped them into his mule-drawn cart.

The mule followed the old man's dog, both animals puffing frosty clouds. Anna's sleepy eyes opened wide as she and Nonna traced her grandmother's girlhood tracks.

Nonna spoke Italian now. "Almost there," she said as the sun exploded on the hill. "Just one more turn."

Anna blinked.

But when the road curved, all she could see were empty garden walls and a hut with no door.

"You said there'd be animals, Nonna!"

"There were — hundreds and hundreds of them!" Nonna's voice trembled. "What happened?"

Then their driver spoke, his cloak still masking his face. "Your grandmother is right, signorina. There were many stone animals. And for a long time after Alfredo died, the zoo was safe, guarded by loyal Papite. Shepherds brought him food, for he seldom left his post.

"But Papite, too, grew old. When he died, the stones began to disappear, and with them, a lifelong dream."

Sighing deeply, the old man left them in the village and drove away.

Cousin Rosa and Cousin Mario greeted them with hugs, and everyone told tales. Anna yawned as the grownups chattered on, but she sat up when Nonna asked about the zoo.

"They say a strange sound can be heard on the hill, when the wind is low. Not the moan of the breeze or a wolf's howl, but a pitiful wail," said Cousin Mario. "Some think it is Papite's ghost calling back his stone flock."

Nonna wept for what she remembered.

That night Anna listened for the wail, but heard only her own breath as she wandered into sleep.

She dreamed of Uncle Alfredo's zoo, of stone turned warm with grunt, whine, whinny, bleat, and caw.

Nonna woke first. "The animals!" she cried, flinging shutters back. "Get up, Anna — it's St. Antuono Day, as I've been telling you! The villagers have brought their animals to church — all decorated with garlands and ribbons, just as I remember. The priest will bless them to keep them safe from harm."

At breakfast Anna asked, "May I take an animal to be blessed?"

"We have none," said Cousin Mario. "Not a scraggy cat!"

"Or shaggy sheep," Cousin Rosa added. "Not a single one."

"Never mind," Nonna told them. "If I know my grandchild, she'll find one."

Anna ran outside. Where would she find an animal to be blessed? Then she saw a pile of stones, and on top was the perfect pet! He would never spot a stray goat or sniff out a newborn lamb, but his brow was as broad as a sheepdog's, and as white.

"I'll call you Papite," Anna said to her stone animal.

Outside the church, some children
laughed at her.

"It's got to be real," said one. "St. Antuono
is the saint of animals, not *stones*!"

"She's from America," another scoffed.
"How would she know?"

Anna turned her face to hide her tears.
But then she dried her eyes.

There *was* a place where a stone dog could
find a home.

From the edge of the village, she could see the deserted zoo, high on the hill. She listened for the wail of Papite's ghost, but heard nothing except the low wind. She started to climb.

When she reached her great-great-uncle's land, Anna set her stone right by the gap where the gate used to be. It was a perfect place for a sheepdog, even one without a flock to watch.

Even one made of stone.

"Ah, the little American," the priest said as he passed. "Weren't you at church with a dog?"

"They said you wouldn't bless him, Father." Anna showed him her sheepdog stone. "They said he had to be real."

"They were mistaken. Stone animals are important, too." The priest smiled. "With just one lovingly chosen stone like yours, Uncle Alfredo's zoo began. Those animals brought joy to generations of children, including me. To us the creatures were real enough. I'll give your dog the blessing."

The priest blessed the stone, then looked tenderly at the doglike head, still and proud as a sentry's. "If I didn't know better, I'd say it was old Papite himself!"

Anna thanked the priest and ran back to the village. She found Nonna with her cousins.

"Come and see my stone dog, Nonna!"

"Soon," her grandmother said. "Right now, old friends are waiting."

That night, Anna listened again for the ghostly wail.

She thought she heard something odd in the growl of the wind as it nipped at the curtains and herded clouds across the snowy peak.

And the next day, when Anna and Nonna climbed the hill to Uncle Alfredo's zoo, here is what they saw:

Cradled in crevices, roosting on
rocks, crouched in crannies, and nestling in
nooks, there were all the stone creatures
of Uncle Alfredo's zoo, just as Nonna
remembered them.

Each villager had something to say about the return of Uncle Alfredo's animals.

"It was the people who took them all those years ago. When they heard that Father had blessed the girl's stone dog, they saw it as a sign from St. Antuono. They regretted what they'd done, and put the stones back."

"It's the little American; she's brought us luck!"

"A miracle!"

All too soon, it was time to go back to America.

At the station, Anna said, "Our driver was the first to tell us about Uncle Alfredo's zoo. Ask *him* about the stones, Nonna."

But when her grandmother turned to speak, the cart was gone.

Up on the hill, a new sound was heard.
Not the moan of the wind or a wolf's howl,
or even the whoosh of the departing train.
  It was light and staccato, like a sheepdog's
joyous bark, or the laughter of a very old man.

*This book is dedicated to Cristofaro, who introduced me
to his uncle's deserted "zoo" outside Frosolone, the village that
inspired the Cantalone of my story. Perched high in the mountains of
central Italy, Frosolone celebrates the festival of St. Antonio Abate
(known locally as St. Antuono) each January seventeenth.
On that day people crowd the church plaza as their garlanded and
beribboned animals receive the priest's blessing.   J.V.*

The illustrations are watercolor, ink, and colored pencil.
The text is set in Palatino.
Designed by Karen Johnson Campbell.

Library of Congress Cataloging-in-Publication Data
Vigna, Judith.
Uncle Alfredo's zoo.
p.   cm.
Summary: Having traveled to a small village in Italy to see an ancestor's
collection of stone animals, Anna is disappointed to find it vanished,
but then one night the animals mysteriously reappear.
ISBN 0-8075-8292-1
[1. Animals — Fiction. 2. Italy — Fiction.] I. Title
PZ7.V67Un 1994   93-19360
[E] — dc20   CIP
                                                        AC